Charlotte, North Carolina

Copyright © 2018 by Gary McPherson.

Dedication

This book is dedicated to the smartest and most fascinating man I ever knew, my father. He was a farmer, carpenter, plumber, real estate genius, business guru, and rocket engineer that helped get us into space and on the moon. Most of all, he proudly called himself a "hillbilly" from Blacksburg, Va. Lucius McCray exists in memory of his humor, intelligence, and wisdom.

To my Wife – Donna McPherson, thank you for believing in me and joining me in this amazing journey called life these past thirty-one years.

Carey Cowan Holman – Thank you for your tremendous editing. Lucius and I remain incredibly grateful.

Lizette and Darren Conover – Your continued encouragement and support have been an inspiration.

Finally, thank you to my readers. May this first book be one of the many that you purchase, and we enjoy together.

Read more stories by Lucius at https://gmacwriter.com/blog-posts/. Click on one of the stories under "Lucius" on the right-hand side.

The Ballad of Pumpkin

I reckon when folks hear the phrase "cat owners" today they think about single, lonely, middle-aged women, or men who like to wear onesies to bed. But back when I was a youngin, cats were considered just this side of feral. Even today, most cats keep a wild streak deep down inside them. Felines don't believe they need to cotton to anybody. If you call a cat it's just as likely to walk away from you as it is to walk to you. The cats I grew up around spent their days killin' birds, killin' mice, or harassin' the dog. I even knew a few cats that hung out in barns and could take out a snake or rat.

That's why, when I got older, I promised myself I would own a cat. Unfortunately, my spouse Darla has always considered cats sort of a disposable animal, to put it politely. Needless to say, I was surprised when she let me get a yellow tomcat for a family pet. He was a right smart lookin' animal and reminded me of one of the cats I grew up with.

Darla only had one condition with me gettin' that kitten. I had to let our kids name it. Now, I figured there weren't any harm in doing that. After all, kids love animals and can come up with the cutest names. I was expectin' somethin' like Fluffy, Cotton Ball, Sir Purr, or even perhaps Needles (on account of his claws.) You can imagine my surprise when my two boys strolled up and proudly announced the name of the cat was Pumpkin.

My boys thought that was a right smart name. After all, Pumpkin was a yellow cat with a bit of white fur on his stomach and a little on his face. Really, he was mostly orange, but I pictured him as a tiger, not a jack-o-lantern.

I must admit, I was fit to be tied. I cajoled, begged, and pleaded for anything but that name. Of course, the boys' mama thought the name was perfect, and that was all the encouragement they needed. I knew right then and there that cat's life was headed for trouble. He grew into a real ornery puss. I am positive, to this day, it was that stupid name that turned that animal almost completely feral.

Even though the boys were about as good to that pussycat as any kids could be, Pumpkin still hated them for some reason. I've seen some mean animals in my day, but Pumpkin pretty much led the pack. If you told him no, he would go over and claw the furniture. If you'd squirt him with water, or swat his hind in with a small newspaper, he'd just run to the other side of the room and claw another piece of furniture. And I won't even get into the issues with him sprayin'.

The battle to domesticate that animal came to a head one day when our two-year-old son was walking across the room.

He wasn't doin' anything but mindin' his own business, not that two-year-old youngins have much business to mind. I reckon that cat felt like he was big enough to express the disapproval of his name. I watched Pumpkin run across the room, jump up in the air, and drag his claw down my son's face. That crazy cat drew blood all the way down my boy's forehead.

Now I know at this point some of you readin' this are thinking I should have taken that cat to the pound or used him for target practice. I will say that you have a point, and Darla was of the same mind set, but to be honest with you, I have a hard time harmin' anythin'. I really do. I have killed a few creatures like spiders, a snake, mice, deer, and coyotes, but I took no joy in it. I love life, and I love all of God's creation. Even if some of it don't love me back.

That old cat had me in a bind though. He broke the cardinal rule: he had hurt one of my sons. Darla was right to want to put him away, but I knew the minute Pumpkin went to the shelter he was a dead tom walkin'. Nobody wants to adopt an animal that's attacked a child. Darla said option two was to remove his claws. Even back in those days that was considered extreme, but versus killin' the animal it seemed merciful. We also got him fixed to mellow out his attitude, and his sprayin'.

Well, we got old Pumpkin home, and he was one mellow pussycat during his recovery. I reckon even the most rambunctious animal is bound to relax with enough drugs in him. We all had a quiet couple of days, and even Darla softened towards him, what with his front claws all bandaged up and such. Unfortunately, that didn't last too long.

The moment that cat felt better, up he went runnin' around the house like a demon had possessed him. He made laps around the livin' room and laps down the hall. Then he'd stop and try and claw the furniture. Of course, that stupid cat didn't seem to understand he didn't have any claws. He'd paw at the base of the couch which made us all laugh at him. I swear to you as surely as I write this, that cat glared at us, and if he could speak English, he would surely have been cursin' at us.

I guess by this point Pumpkin thought it was time to make a bolder statement. He took a running lap around the room and jumped on the back of our old vinyl couch. I believe he intended to stick his claws in and leave scratches and holes all along the top. However, he didn't have any claws. So instead, he went shootin' across that vinyl couch like an egg through a hen. His front legs started to back-peddle but he wasn't slowin' down a lick.

Fortunately, he is still a cat. So, when he came shootin' off the end of the couch he landed on his feet. Well, he might have rolled a few times after that, but he was okay. Now most smart critters, like ants, spiders, opossums, squirrels, they would have realized somethin' was amiss. Not Pumpkin. The darn cat never could figure out his claws were missin'. He spent most of his life tryin' to claw up the furniture, or occasionally one of the youngins, and he never understood why he couldn't make a scratch.

Unfortunately, life's circumstances made Pumpkin's trials and tribulations even harder. We used to live in the city when we were raisin' our kids. In those early years we rented more than a couple places. One day we were movin' from the north side of Charlotte, NC to a nearby town called Matthews. We had friends and co-workers helping us haul our belongings across the city. Finally, the time came to load the kids and the cat in the minivan and say goodbye to the place we'd called home for the last year.

We got everything loaded and I went inside the house and picked up Pumpkin. I reckoned at the time I had a smart plan. I would put the cat in the van, close the door right quick, and then be on our way. I eased the cat on in towards the back row of seats in the minivan, and then closed the door as fast as I could. Unfortunately, old Pumpkin was just as fast. Instead of that door latchin' in place, it sort of bounced out of my hand, and I was convinced I'd just cut my cat in half.

Fortunately, I did not catch Pumpkin in the midsection, but I did manage to catch him in the head. I have to be honest at this point. I don't remember the cat runnin' off, but I do remember holdin' him and prayin' I hadn't killed him. He was lookin' up at me in my arms, his eyes all dazed and glassy and the end of his tongue stickin' out of the front of this mouth. Almost like that old cartoon, "Bill the Cat." He blinked and was breathin' okay. Thanking God for reviving my cat, I put him back inside the van and he walked on into the rear, far away from that door.

That poor fella was never the same after that. Don't get me wrong, he was still one of the meanest cats I have ever had the pleasure of being around. He just didn't seem to know what sort of cat he wanted to be after that. Maybe he became bi-polar. Pumpkin just seemed to be a loving domestic animal one minute, and the next the most bitter feline on four legs.

At the new homestead we rented he used to try and harass the neighbor's dogs. These weren't no little dogs neither. One place had a German Shepherd. Another place had a Golden Retriever. Not the sort of canines that fear cats. At first, I wasn't sure what was goin' on. That cat would disappear, and a few days later come draggin' on home with bite marks and blood, lookin' like he'd had the fight of his life. We'd clean him up, and he'd stay around home for a month or two, and then do it all over again.

Then one day I saw him walkin' across the street towards the house with the German Shepherd and I figured things out. However, when I went to get the cat he shot off across that street and out of sight. It took three days before he came back beat up again. I reckon between his brain damage, and never havin' the sense to know he didn't have claws, that poor tom spent most of his free time receiving butt wuppin's from the neighborhood canines.

Fortunately for Pumpkin, we only lived there a couple of years before we could finally afford to build our own little homestead. By then Pumpkin was approachin' middle age in cat years and finally calmin' down a mite. Of course, his tongue still stuck out of his head, but he was mostly content to lay around the house. At least until we got our Basset Hounds. Now everyone knows that Bassets are the most loveable and smelliest dogs God ever put on this earth. They love people, they love children, and the breed has a weak bite, despite their ferociously deep bark.

That breed was perfect for our three youngins with another on the way. When Pumpkin first met up with them he'd swat at them with his paw when they got too curious, and those puppies would run away cryin'. At first, they were like

Pumpkin and assumed the critter still had his claws. However, the day came with those dogs figured it out. That was the day I learned somethin' about basset hounds. They love to put things in their mouths. That poor cat had more doggy drool on him than an old tennis shoe. If you think a hound dog stinks in the summer, you should try being a cat and havin' 'em slobber on your body sometime.

Now don't get me wrong, those two hound dogs loved that old cat, but the feelin' was most certainly not mutual. After that, Pumpkin spent most of his days out front, or inside the house. He didn't have any use for the backyard with the two long eared, smelly breathed pups. Of course, being Pumpkin, he would forget on occasion, they'd slobber him up proper, and he'd leave in humiliation until the next time.

I realize it may sound like Pumpkin was treated poorly, but that was never the case. The animal had a good life indoors and out. Pumpkin just had a propensity for making poor life choices. Whether it was attackin' toddlers, attackin' furniture, attackin' big dogs, or tryin' to outrun a closing door, he just never seemed capable of figurin' out cause and effect. To be honest, I have some distant relatives that have a lot in common with Pumpkin.

That poor cat met his untimely demise in true Pumpkin style. He used to love to lay on the cool concrete in the garage in the summer time. He'd wait until the car was just entering the garage to hop up and move out of the way. Well, I reckon he was having one of his mental breakdowns the day Darla drove in the garage from the grocery store. He decided he would take on that minivan wheel instead of moving out of its way. Darla came in the house cryin' that she'd hit the cat.

I found old Pumpkin at the front door of the house lookin' for me. His poor back was broken and he was draggin' his rear legs. He gave me a woeful meow all the way to the vet. Fortunately, the vet said his broken back stopped him from feelin' any pain where he was injured. There was nothing they could do and we had to put him down. I was so broken hearted. He was an ornery puss, but he loved me, and I loved him.

They covered him in formaldehyde, wrapped him in a blue tarp, and let me bring him home to bury. I took my grief out on the ground. Unfortunately, our property has what is known as hardpan, or white clay. You can't get any kind of blade through it when it's dry. So, I used a pick and dug for all I was worth.

After going non-stop for a good two hours I had me a hole at least eighteen to twenty inches deep. We laid Pumpkin in his final resting place and covered him up. Since the hole was too shallow for a proper size plant we placed a stepping stone to mark his grave instead. I suppose he's still laying there in peace unless the people living there now move that stepping stone and try to plant somethin'. If they do, I sure hope old Pumpkin don't forget he's dead and his bones go walkin' off.

Lucius Gets Neutered

Several years back Darla and I had a heart to heart discussion about our kids. We had four boys by then, but I kept wantin' a little girl. That was on account of my friends. They all had daughters and I was jealous. Their little girls would snuggle up with their daddy or make him do somethin' silly like pretend to have tea with them. All my boys preferred to wrestle, and I don't mean no Grecko Roman style neither. My little fellas would take a running start, fly through the air, and land knees first into my ribs, back, head, or whatever was vulnerable when I wasn't lookin'. Needless to say, I wanted to add one girl so I'd have a child who could love me without sendin' me to the hospital.

Now Darla didn't find my excuses convincin' for another baby. I can't blame her since I was four and zero when it came to boys vs. girls. We decided at that point we should probably avoid accidently having any more, and that started a whole new debate as to who would go to the vet to get fixed. She told me women have all sort of problems when they get neutered. So, I decided to do the honorable thing and volunteer.

The next step was to make an appointment with the wiener doctor. I guess I should call them urologists since that is their correct title. Whatever their title is, that's one job I don't reckon I could do, even if I have castrated in few bulls in my day.

Back then you had to get approval from your primary doctor for those things. Now normally I prefer female doctors. It ain't because I'm sexist, but I'm less likely to punch a female doctor if she hurts me. I once twisted my rheumatologist's arm away from my sore knee when he wouldn't stop pokin' it. On the other hand, I have a female pain doctor that puts needles into my body and digs around to see how bad I hurt, and I smile while she does it. The male ego is a funny, and stupid, thing.

Since I couldn't decide what wiener doctor I wanted to see, I told my primary doctor that I'd get back to her later with a decision. It was shortly after that phone call I started to notice a disturbing trend. Darla and all her friends would begin to laugh maniacally whenever she told them I was going to get fixed. I had never considered that body part to be a matter of disdain among the fairer sex. It does a few things for us guys. It lets us release our old beer and cold coffee, and occasionally express approval when it sees someone it likes. Other than that, we don't think much of it. In fact, we go out of our way not to look at or talk about it with our buddies. I was a bit worried that every woman thought cutting my tenderest parts was funny. I had no idea they were so bitter about it.

After the Lord showed me that epiphany, I thought it best to go with a male urologist. When the day came to go to the doctor Darla offered to go with me. I thought about all the laughter and decided this was probably best done alone. After all, it was just a consultation. Now I got to say, that consultation was an educational event. First, these urologists have a sense a humor. I reckon you'd have to lookin' at wieners all day. The second thing I learned was there are higher levels of awkwardness I ain't never been exposed to before.

I foolishly assumed we would just sit in the treatment room and chat. After all, we both knew why I was there, and things did start normal. Then old Doc Brown (that's what I'll call him) says, "Mr. McCray, please stand up and drop your pants and underwear."

Now that was a surprise. I had not heard those words since I tried to join the Navy. Of course, I complied, and he rolls on over sittin' on his stool. At this point I was not sure what to do. Part of me wanted to grab my pants and go screamin' out of that patient room. Another part of me wanted to ask for a cup of water so I could put it on his head. He's squeezin', pullin', and liftin'. I felt like a prize bull at the county fair.

After a few more seconds of his probin' I decided to close my eyes and go to my happy place. I go to this real pretty lake on the edge of some woods I like to hike through near Boone, NC. I was just startin' to relax where I hear Doc Brown say, "Give me your finger." I sort of snap back to reality and he repeated, "Lucius, give me your finger." Then, before I can move he's got hold of two of my fingers. Now I'm holdin' my breath prayin' no jazz music starts up. He takes my fingers and pushes against one of my personal parts, and asks, "Do you feel that?"

I says yes because I was praying it was not goin' any farther, but old Doc Brown could tell I was a faker. He adjusts his grip on my finger and says, "No, not that, this." There under my finger was one of the thickest veins I'd ever felt. That changed everything. When you work on a farm you learn to do a lot of your own vet work to save money. In that moment I went from awkward to wonderin' what I was feelin'. "What is that?" I asked.

"That's what I'm cutting in half." He says.

You really must have to have a special kind of dark humor to be a wiener doctor, and I envied the man, but he was not done with me yet. He starts readin' me off options. "If I simply cut it, there is a chance it will grow back together. It happens more often than you think. On the plus side you can reverse the operation later if you choose to. The second option is to cut out a larger section. It's less likely to reattach but is still reversible."

I sat there sort of dumbfounded. I did not want to get my jewels chiseled on just to have things go back the way they were. There was also no chance I would want to reattach the tubes. I asked Doc, "Is there an option that doesn't grow back?"

He crossed his arms and rolled his stool back. I took that as my cue to pull up my pants while I could. He waited for me to finish putting myself together and then said, "I can cut out a section on each side and then clamp a steel ball on the end of each tube. They may eventually fall off one day, but there is no chance you'll ever be able to reattach."

That was the option for me. I said, "Let's do that."

He set me up an appointment for a couple weeks later. Doc Brown also said I would need someone to drive me home after the procedure. I remember how much Darla was enjoyin' all of this, so I knew her givin' me a ride was not a problem. I walked out of his office, a man with a plan.

Now the opinions of the folks I was workin' with was split down the sexes. All the men thought I was either crazy or brave. All the women just laughed. Evidently, vasectomies hit a universal funny bone when it comes to women. Thankfully, I had a male boss at the time. I told him I would be out Friday for the procedure and he promptly doubled over, grabbed himself, and told me to take off as much time as I needed.

The day arrived, and I found myself layin' on a table with my drawers off. Old Doc Brown still had his sense of humor. I love to press a button or two, but this fella had it down to an art. He also had a sadistic streak to go along with it. He stood over me with a razor in his hand, a smile on his face, and asked me if I had shaved things. I told him I trusted a surgeon more since all I owned at the time was a straight razor. I'll just say I was glad he was a good surgeon because he threw that razor around my private parts faster than any man I've seen shave his face. With all the prep work finished, the doctor asked, "What kind of music do you like to listen to?"

Now I may be a country boy, but I have some city in me. In those days I enjoyed all sorts of Rock, including Punk, New Wave, Classic and even some Metal. Needless to say, I didn't think any of those would be appropriate for a man to listen to since he was about to plunge a razor-sharp knife into my tenders. He offered easy listening. Now I ain't no fan of easy listening music, except maybe on a date, but that scalpel was a hair's breath away from my berries, so I was downright agreeable.

I'm sure y'all will thank me for not going into the particulars about my testiculars. Things went along right smooth and Doc Brown seemed to be the master of small talk. The local anesthetic made me forget all about him clipping and sewing down there. My mind started to wander, and so I asked him what his job was like. The good doctor proceeded to tell me about different injuries he had been called on to repair. His ability to verbally paint a picture of a man's disfigured tenders was something to appreciate.

Lookin' back on it, I reckon my lack of revulsion may have been seen as an affront to his story telling. He started on the other side of me not long after he finished his tales of mutilation and horror. First the fella's clamp slipped while he was sticking the needle inside to administer the local anesthetic. I'll be right honest, that hurt a mite. Doctor Brown managed to get his clamp back on and I prayed he did not miss again. Well, everything was moving along better after that. At least until I felt the scalpel.

Now don't get me wrong. It wasn't anything more than a bee sting, but it was inside a part of the body a man does not want stung. Old Doc Brown stopped, grabbed a straight needle and started pokin' at me. He told me to tell him when it hurt, and he confirmed quite a few places weren't numb. He stood there for a few seconds and suddenly exclaimed, "Oh, I'm so dumb. This is a local, I can use the whole thing." He then proceeded to pour the whole container of numbing liquid down the open wound where he was workin'. Thankfully, I couldn't feel a thing after that.

Well, I should day I didn't feel a thing until he started tuggin' and said with a twinge of excitement, "Wow! This is got to be the thickest Vas deferens I've ever had to cut." I wasn't sure if I was supposed to be proud or horrified. I was thinkin' of askin' him if he wanted to go get a sharper pair of scissors when he finally managed to cut through.

Now, have you ever felt like kickin' somebody, but knew if you did you would be worse off for it? I decided after his cuttin' episode I would probably be better off keepin' my eyes closed and talkin' to Jesus. If I didn't and he had more issues down there I might be tempted to work on his tenders with my foot. Thankfully, it wasn't too much longer after that he told me I was done. To my amazement I didn't feel any pain, but I was feelin' weak. The doctor helped me up and had my private parts layin' on some ice and towels.

Of course, Doc Brown was not goin' to let the day end without one more joke. He explained to me that I now officially had balls of steel on account of the clamps left inside. I asked if there was any chance a magnet or metal detector at the airport should set them off. "They shouldn't be a problem," was all he responded with. Then Doc Brown went to get Darla.

Now I'm expectin' her to come in and see what a sacrifice I have made so she didn't have to. I was hopin' for at least a hug after spendin' the last hour with the stand-up comedian/urologist. Well, Darla comes into the room with the doctor followin'. She looks down between my legs and busts out laughing. Our cat Pumpkin got more respect when he got fixed. The whole time Darla is helpin' me ease into my clothes she's gigglin'. I tell you what, that is the sort of reaction that gives a fella a complex.

I was so thankful to get home. I was told to sit in a chair all weekend, watch television, and keep a bag of frozen peas on my broken nuts. They also told me not to walk around too much. I watched television for an hour or so, but then I got bored. I decided I would pass the time by reading over all the documentation they sent me home with. Most of what I read I had already experienced, but then I got into the side effects. Most of the effects revolved around injuring yourself right after surgery, but then I came to the line that said, "Some men may experience a slight shrinkage due to a reduction in fluid." Ol' Doc Brown happily failed to mention that during our consult. In fact, nobody had ever mentioned that. Now to be fair, it almost never happens, but I think that should be the first thing the doctor mentions. I'm guessin' if they made the fact more prevalent their income would drop off precipitously, so they just put it in the fine print instead.

After reading that I felt a mite agitated, so I grabbed my bag of peas and walked outside to get some fresh air and sunshine. That helped me relax. I got bored again after a while, and I decided to take me and my peas into my office, so I could play some video games. Generally speaking, I spent a fair amount of time walkin' around those first couple of days. Of course Darla would follow me around sayin',"Lucius, your doctor said you need to sit. You don't want to hurt yourself." I never went far mind you, just around the homestead. Everything seemed to be progressin' accordin' to plan. I made it up to day two when you are instructed to finally take a shower.

Now, up to this point I had not felt any pain. I thought everything was fine. I will admit I had not looked real close to what the Doc had done because I was afraid I might pass out if I took a good look at it. So, on day two I climbed into the shower. Everything seemed fine until I suddenly felt like a mule had kicked me between my legs. That's when I decided it was time to take a look and see what was wrong.

To my horror I had managed to rip open the stitches, and I thought, *Dang it! Darla was right.* I was seeing inside parts of me I never wanted to see, ever. It took all my strength to fall against the side of the shower and not pass out, or throw up. I start hollerin' for Darla. She comes rushin' in. I'm now in tears looking up at the ceiling. Darla asks, "What's wrong honey!" I point down with my finger and say through my tears, "I tore open my stitches." Darla immediately starts laughing.

At this point any humor I might have ever possessed has long since left me. I holler at her to call the doctor. I'm standin' there naked in shower cryin' when she brings me the phone. The doctor asks me to describe what I see. I attempt to man up and tell him what is going on. His only response is, "Good, don't do anything to it. Take the pain pills I prescribed and pack ice around it."

"You aren't going to sew me back up?" I asked in horror.

"No, just let things drain. If the hole bothers you, you can put a Band-Aid on it." And then he said goodbye and hung up.

Now I've been involved in a few castrations of bulls in my life. I can tell you that we don't just leave things hanging open. Granted, this is not quite the same thing, but we are talkin' similar body parts. To my amazement, pain like a claw hammer hit me tryin' to step out of the tub. Darla had to help lift my leg over the tub because the pain was too much. Then she let me lean on her and got me to the bed. She left and returned with a fresh bag of frozen peas.

I was lying there wearin' nothin' but the jolly green giant's frozen peas, and whimperin' from the pain. Darla seemed to have a little more sympathy and brought me a cup of water and a pain pill. She offered to go to the local CVS and find me somethin' to close up those holes. She didn't appreciate being able to see inside them either. Her sympathy soothed my aching body, up until she started to snicker as she closed the door and the latch clicked shut.

Monday came way too soon. I had promised my boss I would be in to work. Now in those days I worked on computers because I had six mouths to feed. I knew if I could make it to my desk and sit down I could sit there the entire day and type on my keyboard. By I time I drove to the office and showed up at the front door the pain medicine had plumb wore out. I leaned against the door until it opened, and I slowly moved down the hallway towards my desk. The hallway walls were helpin' keep me more or less vertical. Partway down the hall I ran into a bunch of co-workers. They were all a mite concerned for my state of bein'. I was in the mood for some sympathy by this point, and I told them what had happened. The two guys in the group both grabbed at themselves and grimaced. The three women started to laugh. I had never even dated these women, so I'm not sure why they thought my personal affliction was so funny at this point. It isn't even like they could argue they'd been through worse havin' kids since none of 'em was even married yet. Of course, with the laughter and groans a group starts to form to see what's goin' on. Unfortunately, I didn't have the energy to extricate myself from the situation.

Eventually my boss shows up. He sees me leanin' against the wall in pain, and all the women laughin'. The guys are all grabbin' themselves and lookin' at the women in horror and disgust. My boss looks around and says to the women, "It's not funny, everybody back to work." The women walked back into the cube farm where we could hear echoes of laughter for several seconds. A few men gently patted me on the shoulder and told me they were sorry and went about their business.

My boss told me take the week off until I could recover and not to worry about the sick time. I was relieved, until I remembered I had to walk back to my car. That was the longest hundred and fifty yards I have ever walked. Of course, it was the first seventy-five feet to the elevator and the snickerin' from every woman who passed by that was the toughest.

I was back to work after a couple of weeks. My doc had me come in once and confirmed everything had healed up correctly, despite my best effort to mess it all up. Before I left my follow up visit Doc Brown handed me another pamphlet and told me to follow the directions exactly and then bring in a sample to ensure I was as sterile as a steer. I sat in the car and read through what he had given me.

Now I want to try to tell this for polite company. I was told I need to "flush the system" at least thirty times to make sure nothin' was alive was swimmin' about. I smiled all the way home. I walked in the door, walked up to Darla, stuck out the pamphlet and said, "Read this."

"What are you grinning about?" she asked.

"Just read." I said through my smile.

She finished reading it, looked up at me, and said, "You can take care of that yourself."

Now there was a time, in my younger wild days, when I used to think hearin' those words in that context would be excitin'. However, hearing them in real life it sounded more like, "Go mow the grass, and while you're at it, take care of that medical issue."

I'll just say things were takin' care of, but there was one final insult left. The doctor had given me a small plastic bottle to put a sample in and bring into the office. Now they didn't have you bring it into the lab, you just dropped it off inside a brown paper sack with reception. Of course, Darla refused to drop it off. I thought about not havin' the final test done, but by that point I had gone through too much. I had to know if it worked.

So, into the office I went with my bottle in a bag, and I handed it to the pregnant receptionist. My plan was to drop it off and hightail it out the door. I had just turned around on my heel when I hear the receptionist behind me say, "Wait, this only takes a minute in the lab." Thankfully, the waiting room only had a couple of nervous men in it. Most likely Doc Brown's next victims. A nurse called me to the window and gave me a detailed report of what she saw. She must have been able to tell from my blank expression that I had no idea what she was saying, or I was trying not to picture it. The nurse stopped, made sure we had eye contact, and said, "The test came back negative. That means you're sterile." I smiled, said thank you, and got out of there as fast as I possibly could.

I have to say, after goin' through all of this I've never looked at our bull, our steer, or our pet dog without sympathy.

Bathroom Adventures

I guess you can say Darla and I enjoy travelin' right much. We have driven across the United States several times. She joined me on a trip across southern India too. I have also traveled around part of the Southern U.K. as well as New South Wales, Australia, and Guadalajara, Mexico but I did them on business without Darla. I get around alright for a country boy, and for the most part, I have found folks are very similar. We all love our families and want to be treated with respect.

However, I have found when it comes to bathroom facilities, and the people who use those facilities, experiences and preferences vary. Take for instance, the difference between Western toilets and Eastern toilets. Now here in the west, we have ours built for comfortable seatin'. There are seats for youngins, folks that are tall, those who have gone stiff in the knees, and even the bidet. In fact, bidets have started to get so down right popular you can buy them at the Home Depot and simply add them to your toilet. Just make sure you let your company know that it ain't a water fountain.

In the far east, the Japanese have become famous for their bathroom fixtures. They also use bidets, but it's very high tech. Their toilets over there are known for keeping you warm, clean, and fresh. Some even have music hooked up to them. I reckon a fella could find himself fallin' asleep on the toilet if he ain't too careful. I guess you could say I was used to indoor plumbin' in every place I have traveled or thought about travelin'. Although as a young man, I did have an occasion to use an outhouse or two.

Now for the first two weeks I was in India to work, so Darla wasn't with me. Sometimes, without Darla, I miss the forest for the trees. In this case the bidet for the garden hose. Over in India you have three kinds of bathrooms. The first is what folks around here call the European toilet. These "regular" type toilets are in most of the major hotels where westerners stay. The second kind looks like a toilet seat sittin' on the floor with a hole in the middle. This is what the local folks prefer. Finally, when you get out in the country, the fellas just go wherever and whenever they please. It can be sort of a shockin' sight the first time you see it. After a half a day, it don't seem no different than Wobbly stoppin' by a tree. Darla noted later that she never saw the women in countryside usin' the bathroom. I reckon they must only go at night when folks are asleep. That seems like a mighty hard way to live.

I had educated myself on this topic a lot on account of havin' friends who have been missionaries. I had been warned

to make sure there was toilet paper, and there normally was.
However, after spendin' a few days over there you begin to
understand why a billion people find toilet paper
environmentally unfriendly. The hotel staff had mentioned the
bathrooms had bidets, and I was determined to do the right
thing for India and the environment and use mine.
Unfortunately, I was assumin' they meant the toilets that had
those fountains with warm water and soothin' music like
Japan. When I could not find that I started askin' around.

It turns out, the hose that I found hangin' on the wall was
their version of a bidet. Now not meanin' no disrespect on
account of it ain't my house, but I honestly thought the hose
and nozzle were used to clean the bathroom itself. It hung off
to the side on the wall, and it looked like one of those hoses
and nozzles we use in our sinks here in the U.S. The other
reason I assumed it was used for this was due to housekeepin'.
When they left, and I went straight into the bathroom, I found
water all over the place, and there was a drain in the floor. I
just assumed they were hosin' things down like we used to do
the milk barn when I was a kid. I saw the same thing happen
at the office bathroom I was in over there. The cleanin' crew
locked down the bathrooms every hour, and when you walked
back in there was water everywhere, but it appeared clean.

Of course, I wasn't content to let this sort of thing just slip on past me. I was goin' to be visitin' their country for a month, and I wanted to be sure and do the right thing by folks there. I was sure I was just missin' somethin'. Everything over there was a far sight different from home.

Even their architecture was a sight to see. This office they had us workin' in was downright amazin'. Half of it was indoors and half of it was outdoors. You would exit this tiny elevator and be walkin' down this balcony. When you looked up you saw blue sky, but you were still in the office! Now where they kept their computers and such had roofs, but I ain't seen too many buildin's that could include the outdoors as seamless as India. Shoot, our barns can't do as good, and we build them for indoor and outdoor use.

So, I'm walkin' down one of these outdoor hallways with my Indian co-worker Kumar. I have to admit, I'm feelin' pretty ignorant and embarrassed given it is the third day in the country and I still have no idea how to use their toilets. As we are walkin' to a classroom I gently ask Kumar, "Hey, I was told y'all have bidets in your hotels, but I can't find mine."

He stops us and looks at me with a smile that tells me he has been asked this before. I am prayin' he ain't a prankster like me. "Oh, did you not see the hose on the wall?" he asked.

Of course, as soon as he asked me this I felt like a real idiot because I had been commentin' to Darla on email for the first two days about how they wash the bathrooms over there. I decide to go ahead and ask him the obvious question, although I know his answer. "Those are the bidet? To clean yourself with?"

He laughed a little, bobbed his head, and said, "Yes." Over yonder in India they sort of shake their head no to mean yes. It takes some gettin' used to, but It's a hoot when you learn to do it yourself, come back home, and people have no idea why you look like you are sayin' no with your head and tellin' them yes with your mouth. Anyway, I decide when I get back to the hotel I am goin' to use this device and help India's environment like a good visitor.

So, I get back to the hotel, and the moment arrives that I can finally use the bidet on the wall. Well, I can only say things did not work out as I planned. To be fair, it ain't that easy. You really don't want it touchin your body. From behind aiming is sort of opposite from the direction you are thinkin', like backin' up a trailer. From underneath the water falls across your hand and that's just too disgustin' for any more words here. Needless to say, tryin' to find a good angle resulted in my hosin' down that bathroom more than hosin' myself. Well, except for my clothes, they got hosed down right nice. The end of that adventure got my clothes sent to the cleaners. Although I felt bad doin' it, I had to go back to good ol' toilet paper. Well, after that dried out too.

A couple of days after Darla got there we took a train partway across southern India. It was called the Southern Express. We had first class tickets, on account of things bein' so inexpensive thanks to the exchange rate. I have to be honest on this one. I think the train car was first class on account of it having sealed windows, air conditioning, and then backup fans for when the air conditioner could not keep up. The seats sort of reminded me of what you'd see on a school bus here. The folks runnin' the train made up for that though. The service was outstanding. All the people over there are right nice, everyone we met anyway.

So, we're travelin' along our five-hour ride, and of course I need to get rid of some tea I drank earlier that mornin'. Now I assumed the bathroom would be "European", as they called 'em, since it was first class. When I got to the bathroom I found out I was mistaken. There was a toilet lookin' seat, and lookin' through the hole I could see the railroad ties zoomin' by. I reckon not too many kids play on the train tracks over there. I also noticed there was not any hose, not that I needed one for why I was there.

Now that worried me on account of there being two choices over yonder for bathroom hygiene. One is the hose. The second choice instead of a hose or toilet paper is the left hand. I reckon there aren't any left-handed people in India. That's why you always shake and eat with your right hand when you visit their country. Now that may sound a bit gross, but if you've ever been huntin' or stuck out in a farm field and nature comes callin' with no leaf litter in sight a fella will do what a fella has to do. So, it ain't like it's never been done anywhere else.

As I straddled this hole I figured it couldn't be no harder hittin' it than the games we used to play in the bathrooms as kids. Of course, my mother did fuss at me for missin', so it might not be as easy as all that. Anyway, everything was going pretty good. I was at least missin' my pants leg, and that really was what I was worried about the most. Of course, then the train started around a curve and the car started to lurch a bit. By instinct I grabbed the pipes since there were no hand rails to speak of. Although I did not see anything, I knew that was probably not a good move. I must've used almost a full bottle of the alcohol hand cleaner when I got back to my seat.

Well, a little bit later Darla has to go. I warn her about my adventure and ask her if she thinks she thinks she can hold it for the last two hours. Darla gives me one of those looks that makes a fella feel stupid for bein' a man. She gets up and starts down the opposite direction of the bathroom. "Hey, I holler, the bathroom is up yonder."

She just gives me her cute condescending smile and says, "Trust me."

She's gone for a while, and I'm hopin' she hasn't fallen off the train. All of a sudden, from up behind me there she is. As she is sittin' down I'm pullin' out antiseptic, alcohol hand cleaner, and a clean towel from our carry on, but she just takes a small amount of hand cleaner and says she's good.

"Did you find another bathroom that actually has a sink?" I asked her.

She gave me another one of her smiles and said, "I found the European bathroom."

I just shake my head. I did not have to go one more time the entire trip, and to be honest, I felt a bit cheated not gettin' to use the other bathroom.

Now you may be thinkin' at this point in my story, "Lucius, that's a pretty traumatic bathroom adventure," and I would say you are correct. However, we have had two incidents here in the good ol' U.S. of A. One I rank on par with our trip halfway around the world, and the other I believe takes first place above all of this.

Now Darla's folks live out west near Albuquerque, New Mexico. No disrespect to the folks out there, but there ain't nothin' in New Mexico if you're drivin' I-40. Now, I know that will offend some folks, and I have had some conversations about my opinions. But you need to understand, I like the color green when it comes to the outdoors. New Mexico along I-40 is best described as brown with patches of yellow. Now, northern New Mexico is beautiful. You'll see right much if you go up into northern New Mexico towards Colorado. Towns like Santa Fe and Taos are worth the drive to visit. Unfortunately, my in-laws live east of Albuquerque on the only green mountain in the area, and it ain't all green.

So, I try to make an annual drive out there every three to five years. We prefer drivin' because it allows Darla and I to enjoy seein' the different states, meetin' new folks, and enjoyin' the scenery. In our younger days we used to just drive straight through Arkansas without stoppin'. We did this because Tennessee is one of the longest states to drive across, and Arkansas isn't that far across. However, as we have gotten older we need to stop more, and so we found ourselves for the first time in an Arkansas rest area a few years ago. I go walkin' into the men's room. It has the usual non-descript off white tiling on the walls, and even the floors. I notice three stainless steel sinks as I'm walkin' to the stalls. They look familiar, but I think they're unusual because most places use white enamel. I just figure the décor is different on account of us crossin' west of the Mississippi River. Then I walk into the stall.

There in front of me is a stainless-steel toilet, but it ain't no ordinary stainless-steel toilet. I recognize it on account of it missin' a seat, or rather the seat is built into a one-piece bowl. I start to hyperventilate and have flashbacks of the county jail, and then I done forgot the reason I was even in the bathroom. So, I made a quick exit outside. I am breathin' clean free air when Darla comes walkin' out from the ladies room. "Did you notice the bathrooms? They remind me of that time you were in the county jail," she said.

I just nod my head and that's when she notices the sweat on my forehead and the fear in my eyes. I am expectin' at least a little sympathy, but she doubles over, slaps her thighs and just starts hollerin' laughin'.

"I'm glad you think it's funny, woman. I can't even use the bathroom." Darla quit laughin' on account of seein' how heated I had gotten.

"Lucius," she said in a stern voice. "You march your butt into that bathroom and do what you have to do. We need to get to my parents, and I don't want to be late because we have to stop at some McDonalds just so you can pee."

Needless to say, I felt just like a little child. So, I skulked on back into that bathroom, did what I had to do while the sound of the water against metal sent shivers down my spine. I skulked back out with my lower lip sticking out and walked on back to my car like a man.

But none of these adventures, not a one, come close to Oklahoma and a Love's Travel Stop. Now most fellas of my generation grew up learnin' some simple rules about the bathroom.

The first rule is that you never look down if another fella is in the bathroom with you. Don't worry, you won't fall, we keep our floors clear so we don't have to look down. The second rule is never speak to each other. Nobody wants to hear that you and your buddy are goin' to have a pig pickin' unless we are all invited. These seem simple enough to follow. They also should be simple enough to translate into other actions in the bathroom. For instance, talkin' on a cellphone, or talkin' to yourself would be included in being quiet.

Now if you travel, you know most truck stops cater to cars as well as truckers. They are great places to stop and use the bathroom, grab some food, and fuel. Most, but not all the time, the bathrooms are clean and large. So, we decided to pull off at a Love's Travel Stop in the middle of nowhere

Oklahoma. Darla goes her way and I go mine. To my surprise, there isn't anyone in the men's room. Now I was not worried, since it was a Sunday and later in the mornin' when most folks are either in church or already on the road. I open the red stall door and go on inside. I'm happy to see the stalls are very private with actual walls between them. The urinals are on the opposite wall. The stall door has the normal cracks around, but nothing too bad.

I'm just about finished with things when this fella walks in. He is as lanky a man as I have ever seen. He looked to be around six-foot-tall, not counting the straw cowboy hat that seemed to shade his entire skinny body. He walks up to the urinal directly across from my stall. I'm about to get situated to leave when I see him do something unexpected.

He puts his hands up against the wall above his head like he's gonna be frisked by the police. He appears to be lookin' down at his sticks and berries and I'm thinkin' that fella is gonna wet himself. Nothin' is happenin' and I'm beginin' to wonder if he has a medical problem. All of a sudden, he starts singin'. Except, he ain't singin' words, or hummin a tune. He's just sort of starts singing a tune like cowboys do in movies when they are alone on the prairie. Next thing I know, I hear his water works start up. Now at this point I think it must be his way with dealin' of relievin' himself at the urinal, except this fella keeps singin' while lookin' down at himself.

I don't mind tellin' you, by this point I'm feelin' a bit nervous. I decide it's probably best to stay behind my locked door and wait for him to leave. Even after the sound of runnin' water stopped this fella just kept singin'. By this point I was feelin' a bit panicked and prayed somebody else would be walkin' in soon, but there wasn't nobody else. He finally gets done with his tune, lets go of the wall, zips up, washes up, and walks out. I'm still not sure I want to leave the stall, but a minute later two more fellas come walkin' in. Feelin' a bit more secure I come on out, wash up, and get to my truck and Darla as fast as I can.

I have been privileged to see a lot of this world, meet a lot of great folks, and use a lot of bathrooms. You can believe me when I tell you I have many more adventures I could add in here, but then it would no longer be a short story. Even if I did add every story I have, there ain't anybody, or any place, on the globe that will ever beat the singin' cowboy at the Love's Travel Stop.

A Tale of Wobbly

I've had my dog Wobbly for some time now. He's not half as goofy as he used to be, and I have to be honest, he's a right homely lookin' pet. The front half of him looks like a bulldog, but his back-half is mostly Basset Hound. His gray head and tri-colored body look like somebody went and sewed two dogs into one. Wobbly's large tongue is as wide as it is long. That thing just hangs out of his mouth below his double chin droppin' slobbers everywhere he walks. He has left our house in an awful mess. Darla spends half her day mopping up dried doggy drool, and the other half cussin' because Wobbly has already messed up her floor again. Of course, his good looks and slobberin' habits are exceeded only by his natural odor. That animal could gag a maggot on a warm humid day, but we don't blame Wobbly because he's a hound dog, bless his heart.

Now you may be wonderin' why we don't keep him outside in a kennel. We used to do that with our early dogs. We learned over the years that the weather and predators make life downright miserable for a dog caged up outside. Then there's the barkin'. There ain't nothin' more heart breakin' than a dog cryin' for his family. We adopted Wobbly, slobbers, smells and all, so he lives inside with us.

Besides, he is a sight to behold when a stranger comes wanderin' around. Just yesterday we had a neighbor boy that liked to cut through our backyard to get to his buddy's house. Now I don't mind that none as I used to do it when I was a youngin', too. I had just let Wobbly out in the backyard to play. Even though we don't have a fence Wobbly enjoys staying inside the boundary of his own yard. I reckon that's the bulldog in him because a Basset Hound will run away for miles if you don't keep them penned up. Anyway, this young man comes strollin' along into our yard. Now Wobbly wasn't angry. In fact, I think he likely wanted to play. So, Wobbly goes galloping with his short legs and long body towards that boy. Now what that young man saw was Wobbly's big head bobbin' up and down, tongue slappin' his face and spit flyin' everywhere. Ole Wobbly stopped a couple feet away with his crooked tail just a waggin'. To be honest, it looks more like he has a twitch, but that's how he wags his tail.

Now for all of Wobbly's unfortunate genetics he has been given one mighty gift by his Creator. His bark is so low and loud you'd swear I had a Wolf Hound hidden somewhere on my property, and that's his happy bark. Well, Wobbly let out a couple of happy barks to his new friend. That kid screamed, turned tail and run. Of course, Wobbly thought they were playin' a game and chased after him. That kid ran screamin' until he was plumb out of sight. Thankfully, Wobbly stopped at the edge of his yard, because he's as smart as he is ugly. Bless his heart.

Wobbly felt rejected when he realized his new friend wasn't comin' back. He sat out there at the edge of the yard makin' the most awful racket you ever did hear. He even had me tearin' up. When I couldn't take anymore, I headed outside to comfort the little guy. Darla made some joke about me bein' an old softie, but if you would've heard Wobbly you'd done the same. I sat down in the grass and that dog immediately changed his mood and came runnin' for me. That's when I realized I may have made a mistake.

Wobbly had a big grin on that giant head of his. His tongue slapped his face in rhythm with his head as he came runnin' for me. He mouth was shootin' out so much spit he looked like a hairy sprinkler. I was about to stand up, but he was already on top of me. All I could see was his huge pink tongue licking me. Occasionally his long dog ears would slap me in the cheek, and then more tongue and slobber would follow suit. I tried to protect myself by quickly rollin' onto my stomach. That only made the situation worse.

The next thing I know my hair is full of Wobbly slobbers, and he's standing on my back with those short legs. Now that may not sound too bad, but he's full grown now and around sixty pounds. I thought I had four poles tryin' to poke through my back. The moment I started to turn my head my face was fully covered in pink wet dog tongue. He had me completely cornered.

I was relieved to hear the back door open. I knew Darla would come and rescue me from the pounds of puppy love I was experiencin'. I could hardly hear her for the dog tongue sloppin' on my ear.

Somewhere between the squishin' noise I heard Darla holler, "That's what you get, Lucius! You made your bed, now lie it." Then she laughed and went back inside. She sure does like seeing Wobbly and me have fun together. Bless her heart.

I laid there until Wobbly finished givin' me a good tongue lashin'. Thankfully he got bored after another four or five minutes. I was drippin' in dog drool by the time he jumped off my back and sat down waitin' for me to get up. My hair was stuck firmly to my head like I had just covered it in a can of mousse. That could have been right stylish except for the dried bubbles, and bits of things I did not want to think about.

Wobbly and I headed back in the house. Darla gave him a treat, and I gave myself a shower. I felt a lot better once I was all cleaned up. I walked into the family room, and Darla was relaxin' in her recliner and Wobbly was entertaining himself with a rope I had tied to an iron ring I had bolted into the fireplace. I sat down ready to recover from the day's activities.

I had just grabbed the television remote when Darla spoke up.

"We are down three more hens," she said.

I knew what that meant. We had coyotes again. Coyotes had killed our other dog. They had taken out two hens and I decided to lock the biddies in the hen house. I had put Flash in the fenced pen. There was a small opening that only a single animal could get through at a time. I figured the coyotes would be smart enough not to take on Flash one at a time. Unfortunately, they were smarter than I thought. They had coaxed Flash out of the pen instead. He was severely outnumbered and never had a chance. They had not been around since.

Darla sat there lookin' at me waitin' for a response. I knew Wobbly would be no match, but the two of us together might make a fight of it.

I turned to Darla and said, "Well, I suppose my rifle and Wobbly's bark just might make those scoundrels think twice about comin' around here again."

Darla grunted and went back to readin'.

I got up and got my trusty huntin' rifle. My .30-06 had never failed me. I've killed coyote and bear, as well as deer with it. This gun has saved my life on more than one occasion hiking through the woods. My rifle may look beat up and worn around the wooden stock, but her barrel is well oiled and loved as well as I love my dog. Now the three of us were going to put an end to that pack of killers.

The dog, my gun, and I all headed out the door. I heard Darla yell, "Be careful with Wobbly!" as I shut the door behind us. I hefted Wobbly up into my pickup, put my rifle in its rack and headed down to the farm as the sun was startin' to go down. It was goin' to be a cold night, so I brought along a thermos of hot coffee for me, and some warm water for Wobbly.

The farm felt cold and desolate when I pulled up next to the hen house. Normally this was my sanctuary, but it had been invaded by a pack of killers, and I was sure they were watchin' me unload Wobbly from the truck. I had no doubt they were sizing up their odds for when the sun fell below the horizon. I came prepared though. From behind my truck seat I pulled out night goggles. When the time came I would see as good as those scrounges.

Wobbly followed me to the back of the pickup and I got a folding chair. We got to the fence and I unfolded the chair next to the small opening in the fence. If worse came to worst, I'd push Wobbly through the opening and make my stand there alone. But, it was not nightfall yet. I decided to have some fun with the hens. I put Wobbly on his leash, opened the gate and let him bark at the biddies. Oh, Lord you ain't never seen such a sight. Feathers and wings were flyin' everywhere as they fought each other to get in that hen house.

Lookin' back on it I guess that was a mite cruel considerin' a coyote had just killed a couple of their friends, but at the time I was just needin' a distraction. I got Wobbly quiet when the last one dashed inside and closed the door to the hen house. There was nothin' to do now but wait.

It was 11 pm and I had finished half my thermos. Wobbly was curled up under my chair tryin' to stay warm and snorin' up a storm. In fact, he snored so loud I didn't recognize his growl. I felt him bump against my chair and knew he was no longer sleepin'. That's when the first howl came from the edge of the woods a short way down the field. There's somethin' about a coyote howl that will put a chill through your bones. When the pack answers the chill will cut all the way through your body.

I pulled down my night goggles and looked around. I still did not see them. I looked down as I felt Wobbly walk out from under me. I had never seen him really angry before then. All his hair was standin' up. His sagging shoulders now rippled with muscles. His tongue was no longer hangin' out. He was sniffin' the air and those large jaws flexed in anticipation.

To my surprise four coyotes appeared at the same time out of the forest's edge, but they were spread apart. The alpha was not hard to spot. He stood a good six inches taller than the others and was in the center with one on his left and two on his right. The three females started to walk diagonally, likely hopin' to distract my attention away from the alpha-male by movin' to one side or the other. That alpha was bold. He just kept walkin' slowly straight ahead. Wobbly took a half dozen steps towards him.

I called, but Wobbly would not respond. I knew then what they intended to do. They would pull the dog away and me with him when I stepped out to retrieve him. Then it was just a matter of circling both of us. My one chance was to shoot the alpha first and pray I had enough time to kill or wound another two before they were on us. I began to raise my rifle, but I was too slow. The alpha began his charge. To my surprise Wobbly found his legs and took off like a shot.

If I shot my rifle now I risked hitting Wobbly, and my heart would not let me take that risk. I prayed for a miracle. Wobbly and the alpha met with such force they both rolled over each other on the ground. When the somersaults had stopped, Wobbly ended up on top, his massive jaws locked on the coyote's throat. Blood was flowin' across Wobbly's lips and he showed no signs of letting go. That alpha regained his legs and stood up, but the bulldog in Wobbly had come out. Nothing was going to release Wobbly's grip. The more that coyote tried to shake Wobbly loose, the more he cut his own throat.

It was then I noticed movement on my left. Two of the coyotes realized things were not going as planned and were headed for Wobbly. I raised my gun and took each one down with a single shot. I turned to my right to see the third coyote lookin' and me and slowly backin' up towards the woods. I turned back to see the alpha lying still on the ground, and Wobbly with him. I turned my gun back to the fourth coyote, but it had disappeared.

I finally felt like I could breathe again. I walked over to Wobbly. I could see through my night goggles he was breathin' hard. His nose was movin' back and forth as fast as he could manage to try and get in all the air he possibly could. I called his name and his eye shot up and looked at me.

"It's okay, boy. We got 'em," I said.

Wobbly finally relaxed his jaw. He slowly got back up on his legs and stretched his sore body. He shook his massive head and slobber and blood got on my legs, the end of my gun, and my hand. He was fine. I wiped the blood off my hand, pulled out my cell phone and called for the Sheriff to send someone to pick up the dead coyotes. We had to confirm none of these varmints had rabies.

Now as I tell some folks, the Sheriff and I don't always see eye to eye, but when it comes to wildlife and rabies we are always in agreement. He showed up with animal control about a half hour later. Wobbly and I were enjoyin' our last bit of warm liquid. The animal control officer asked me if Wobbly was up to date for rabies and I showed him his tag. I warned them one got away. I was sad to hear several farmers had been havin' trouble with more than one coyote pack. I reckoned it was time we thought about startin' up a hunt soon. The Sheriff offered to set that up for me. I'm still thinkin' about that one. I'm not sure I trust that man around me with a gun in the woods.

Well, the two of them got busy with the dead coyotes and I got out of their way. I decided to leave the hens locked up for the night in case that last coyote decided to try its luck after we'd left. After the Sheriff got done walkin' around the killed animals he came over to me and ran his flashlight over us. That's when he noticed Wobbly's dried drool on my shoes and jeans. He also noticed the coyote blood mixed in. He shined the flashlight on his face. I couldn't help but notice a look of pity in his eyes and a slight smile in the corner of his mouth as he spoke to me. "Lucius, you know the protocol if we don't know if a wild animal has rabies."

I didn't like where he was headin'. "I know, but these coyotes didn't appear rabid. In fact, they were so smart and coordinated it was downright scary."

"You said the male charged you and Wobbly, even though Wobbly's a dog and you had a gun."

I sighed. I knew exactly what was comin'. "I'm sorry, but we need to take you to the hospital and get the shots started."

"But to blood came off Wobbly's slobbers!" I protested.

The Sheriff put his hand on my shoulder, "I'm sorry, Lucius. Wobbly's had his shots. You haven't. I'm just tryin' to keep you alive."

I knew I was defeated. "You and Wobbly. Bless y'all's hearts."

At least the Sheriff called the vet. He came on out,
picked up Wobbly and took him back to his office to get him
cleaned him up proper. That allowed Darla to come directly to
the hospital. She walked into my room with a worried look
and then shook her head like I should've known better.

Even though I'm sittin' here in the hospital with an arm
full of needle holes, I'm right proud of Wobbly. He can be as
dangerous as he is homely, and that makes him a right decent
guard dog.

The Fall Moonshine Run

It was an early Saturday mornin'. The sun was just startin' to turn the gray sky to blue. I had just finished packin' up the last load of shine. This load would be delivered to a friend of mine up in Clemmons, NC. I had put together a nice mash with apples and honey inside it. It tasted so good I kept an extra six quarts for myself. It would come in handy when the weather got colder.

The old copper still had sat next to the North Fork Edisto River all season long. I had her up in the woods, away from pryin' eyes. I hated to see this season end. I knew I would not be usin' this spot again for a long time. I loved this location. A breeze ran past the still most evenings when I would wander out this way. You could hear the frogs and crickets in the summertime. Without any houses around to light the sky the stars would go on forever.

This was my location to get close to God. Even without my still, it's my favorite place in South Carolina to come and think about things. The fella that owns the land is a friend of mine, and he knows I'd never harm anything. Just like the last time when I used this location, I intend to return and break down my equipment, load up all my belongin's and take them back to the barn. When I have everything cleaned up this spot will look prettier than the day I started brewin'. I just had to complete this one last delivery.

I knew goin' across state lines was a dangerous game. When you run moonshine to your neighbors' homes you're less likely to run into trouble. The police are not always in the mood to take you in on account of you deliverin' your product to their neighbors, or kin. Makin' deliveries is even easier if the cops, or the mayor, are customers. However, if you head across state lines they are not as understandin'. North Carolina is especially nasty because of their government run ABC cartel. Those folks keep a strangle hold on any and all alcohol bein' sold in the state. If they find you shinin' they won't hesitate to throw you in jail and make an example out of you to other moonshiners who might try and come into their state.

I slowly drove my old 4x4 pickup truck down through the woods, across my buddy's field, up past his barn, and onto the road. The sun had finally made its way up past the tree line. I was headin' north on 601. The trees and grass were still green, but the taste of early fall was in the air. The longer mornin' shadows off the trees reminded me cooler weather was close at hand.

I wanted to avoid the interstates. I wasn't worried none about the police findin' my shine as long as I was not involved in any sort of wrecks. Takin' the smaller highway and slower speed would be the safer route, and it was a fair bit prettier.

Now, I love my old truck. She has been faithful to me for over thirty years. I painted her gray five years ago so we wouldn't draw too much attention together. I was lookin' forward to the drive. The country roads were mostly empty and the air had just enough bite to make it worthwhile to roll down my window. Everything was perfect as I got into the next county, but ten minutes later I saw a deputy behind me with his lights on. I looked down at my speedometer. Sure enough, I was driving just under. I pulled on over figurin' he would go right on by, but son of a gun, he pulled in behind me.

He asked for my license and registration. His name plate said Officer Odell.

"Do you know why I stopped you?" Odell asked.

"No, sir." I could answer right honestly.

He smiled, bent down, and looked under my truck. I could feel my butt cheeks gettin' a little tighter. I had hid my friend's shine in a spare gas tank. Actually, it only looks like a gas tank. It's always used to haul my moonshine if folks need more than a few quarts.

Officer Odell handed me back my license. "Looks like you've got a leak," he said. "From the smell of it I believe it's apples. I don't suppose you want to explain that to me."

Now, being an old country boy, this was not my first rodeo. "Absolutely, officer. I have a buddy who makes ethanol. He was low on corn and wanted to see how apples would work. I'm testin' it out for him in my old truck."

"Uh-huh," was all Officer Odell would say. He took off his glasses and looked straight into my eyes with his baby blues. "Mr. McCray. Let me make this quick because I don't know how big your leak is. I think I know a relative of yours who goes by the name Marcus Johnson."

I smile because I believe I know where this is headed, and I begin to nod my head slowly.

The officer smiled back and continued, "Good. I have some tape in my patrol car that should fix your leak. I'm willing to help out if you are willing to share some of your "ethanol" with me."

Well, who am I to say no? Especially when an officer is kind enough to help me fix my leak. He goes back to his patrol car and gets his gorilla tape. I crawl under and tape off the crack that evidently happened when I was drivin' over the rocks out of the riverbed. I crawled back out from under the truck, open my door, reached behind the seat, and gave Officer Odell one of the six quarts I had kept for myself.

I said, "Much obliged."

The officer took off the lid, took a sip and smiled. "You drive safe now." He said as he screwed the lid back on. "Don't let anyone else catch you with that ethanol. They may not be so understanding."

I thanked him for his advice and started back on the road after he left me. The drive was still beautiful, and God was showin' me His mercies. After all, if the deputy hadn't pulled me over I wouldn't have known my shine was leakin' out of my secret tank. If that had kept up I was liable to be plumb dry by the time I got where I was goin', and my friend would be powerfully disappointed.

The sky was a beautiful Carolina blue as I pulled into the south end of Mocksville, NC. I had been cruisin' at a cool fifty miles per hour most of the trip. I didn't have too much further to go when I passed a police car parked near Mocksville Motors. I waved as I went by, and he smiled and waved back. As I went on by I noticed the black and white police cruiser turned his lights on. I reckoned he had a call come, and so I slow down and look to see which direction he is headed. When I see him turn right I pull on over out of his way. To my surprise the fella pulled in right behind me.

Now if this were back home I wouldn't be worried none. Even my Sheriff will let me off with a warnin' after takin' my shine for safe keepin', but I was well out of state. The officer walked up and I have my window already rolled down and both my hands on the steerin' wheel. I glanced at his badge. "Officer Alex McCoy, good mornin' to you sir."

He smiled and sort of looked past me into my cab. "Good morning. I need your license and registration please."

Of course, I complied, and he left for a few minutes and then came back. He had a pair of gloves on and a piece of paper. "Do you know why I stopped you?" he asked.

I shook my head, "No sir. I thought I was drivin' right neighborly through your town."

Alex nodded, "You were, but unfortunately, the speed limit drops to 45 and you were drivin' 50."

I smacked the steerin' wheel, and the officer reached towards his gun. I slowed down and said, "I apologize, I didn't see that speed limit sign. I promise it won't happen again."

Alex smiled, nodded and then handed me a warnin' ticket. "I know it won't. This is just a little piece of paper to remind you. By the way, Mr. McCray, did you know your left rear tire is almost flat?"

That was news to me, and explained why the truck felt squishy to drive, even with a full tank of shine in the bottom of it. I decided to answer honestly, and hopefully get the officer on his way. "No, sir. I can get out and fix that right after you leave. I have a spare under the truck bed."

Alex said, "Go ahead and step out, and I'll give you a hand."

I suppose he was one of those officers who does protect and serve. He offered to lay down a few flares, and I got the jack and tools out of the back of the cab before he could see my jars. Alex met me at the tailgate while I was crankin' down the spare from underneath the truck bed. As soon as it was down he offered to loosen the lug nuts before I jacked up the truck. He was right neighborly and very handy with that old tire.

I had just slipped off the flat tire when Officer McCoy says, "Do you smell that?"

"What?" I ask.

"Smells sort of like apples, or something sweet."

I smile and scratch the back of my neck while I try and come up with an answer. "Well, I did drive through my neighbor's apple orchard this mornin' We had been out there workin' last night puttin' apples in the truck and then unloadin' where he stores them on the farm. I reckon that's what you're smellin'."

Officer Alex stuck his head over into the bed of the truck, sniffed, shook his head, but kept right on workin'. I was hopin' all this work was takin' his mind off where that smell could be comin' from. I tossed the flat into the bed of the truck after Alex lowered the truck back down. Then Officer McCoy started walkin' towards the cab of the truck.

I put out my hands and said, "Let me take those. I know where they go."

The officer smiled, "That's alright, Lucius. I have an old pickup just like this at home. It used to belong to my dad."

Well I knew I was about to be in a whole lot of trouble. If he moved that blanket at all he was going to find my last five quarts of beautiful apple honey moonshine. I hear him workin' around in the back of my cab, but I'm not goin' anywhere near it. I'm thinkin' at this point it might be wiser to give Officer McCoy all the room he wants. I pretend to be busy checking the spare tire chain under the truck. When I stand up Alex is standing there with a clear Mason jar in his hand, and a right serious look on his face.

"Lucius, tell me something, buddy. Is this what I think it is?"

I was caught red handed. I just prayed Officer McCoy would be a merciful man. I responded, "I guess that depends. Do you think it's water?"

Alex just slowly shook his head no. It was obvious he was not in the mood to play, but I wanted to keep things lighthearted. "Well then, it's probably exactly what you think it is."

Officer McCoy asked me, "Are you up here to sell this?"

"No." I answered truthfully. "Those jars are all that's left. I was keepin' them for me. I'm just up here visitin' an old friend around Clemmons."

Alex gave me a right skeptical look, and opened the jar. He swirled it around a little bit, smelled it, and to my surprise took a sip. He closed his eyes for a few seconds and then a smile came across his lips. He twisted the top back on, and said, "You know I should haul you on in for this. There's enough shine back here to distribute, but I believe you. This is some of the best homemade liquor I have come across in a long time. If I had made this, I'd keep it too. So here's what I am proposing. You put four of those jars in the trunk of my cruiser and we'll call it even."

Before I could stop my mouth from talkin' I answered, "But that only leaves me with one."

Alex frowned. Then he answered in a more serious tone, "Well, the second option is that I take all your liquor and haul you off to jail."

I didn't allow my mouth to open now until I was ready. "Officer McCoy, please allow me to help load your liquor into the trunk of your car."

With a simple nod of his head officer McCoy passed on by me holdin' that first mason jar like it was his newborn son. He had the trunk open as I grabbed the other three and took them on over to him. He kindly advised me to hide that last quart under the passenger seat, and then waited for me to pull back out on the road. I watched him do a U-turn and head the other direction. Although the officer's fee was high, I was thankful to he showed me that tire before it started to shred. That could have caused all sorts of havoc.

The rest of the trip up into Clemmons went on without incident. I met my buddy Blake a piece off Center Grove Church Road at his house. I knew he liked what I had brought him when he started to siphon it out of the tank but drank down a fair amount before lettin' it empty it into his clean buckets. He paid me my askin' price, but then shared some of it with me as well. Needless to say, I had to stay a fair amount longer than I had anticipated. Darla finally called me and said I should get on home.

I said my goodbyes and hit the road. My old truck drove a lot lighter now that the liquor was out of the tank. I took that old pickup, got on the interstate and practically bounced all the way home. I pulled in the driveway as the sun was just below the horizon. I was happy to see that Darla had remembered to leave the porch light on for me. I fished out my remaining mason jar and headed to the house.

As soon as I opened the door Wobbly met me and promptly slobbered all over my work boots. I guess I still had the taste of apples from the still because that dog would hardly let me take a step before he was lickin' those boots. Once Darla thought I had had enough, she called Wobbly into the kitchen and gave him a piece of bacon she was cookin'. I walked on in to say hello.

She took one look at me and said, "Where's the other jars?"

I shook my head. "It's a long story, but I guess the good Lord only thought I needed one quart for this winter."

Darla looked back down at what she was cookin' and said, "Good. Put that in the pantry and don't open it before Christmas."

I nodded, walked into the pantry, quietly unscrewed the lid, took a long sip, and then put it away. A person should enjoy the fruits of their labor after all. I walked back out of the pantry with a smile on my face.

Darla took one look at me and said, "I know what you were doing in there. You be good."

I smiled, went into the livin' room, sat in my chair, turned on the television and hollered over my shoulder, "It's y'all be good!"